I SPY

Colours in Art

For Walter and Molly

FOREWORD

When my children were very young we sorted my collection of fine art postcards into numerous categories - happy pictures, sad pictures, noisy pictures, pictures with dogs or doves or cats or funny hats. We filled a large photo album in which each spread represented a letter of the alphabet and it was this album that eventually became my first art book, I Spy an Alphabet in Art.

I realised early on that my children were learning a great deal simply by looking. They didn't know the names of the artists but they could recognise the wonky eyes in a Picasso or the quality of light in a Caravaggio. We talked about the paintings as if they were ordinary pictures in a picture book, finding funny details, colours, shapes; but also we found myths and legends, bible stories, scenes from all over the world and throughout history. It occurred to me then that if every child in every home and every classroom could be introduced to art (by means of just a few paintings), then they would all grow up with access to this amazing source of knowledge and inspiration.

My children, now grown-up, have helped me to choose the pictures for I Spy Colours in Art. There's plenty to talk about. As well as the colours, there are shapes to find and elephants to count; there is a hairy caterpillar, a young boy in a dress, a boiled egg for breakfast and, of course, some of Picasso's wonky eyes.

Lucy Micklethwait 2006

Cover picture: Robert Delaunay, *Rythme No.1*
Title page picture: Richard Paul Lohse, *Movement around a Four-squared Centre*

I SPY
Colours in Art

Devised & selected by Lucy Micklethwait

HarperCollins *Children's Books*

I spy
with my little eye

a red key

Michael Craig-Martin, *Untitled*

I spy
with my little eye

a yellow
circle

Robert Delaunay, *Rythme No.1*

I spy
with my little eye

two blue
eyes

Pablo Picasso, *Maya with a Doll*

I spy
with my little eye

an orange
orange

John Frederick Peto, *The Poor Man's Store*

I spy
with my little eye

a purple
square

Richard Paul Lohse, *Movement around a Four-squared Centre*

I spy
with my little eye

a green elephant

The fabulous region of Himavant from a Burmese manuscript

I spy
with my little eye

grey smoke

Ando Hiroshige, *Fuji from the Sagami River*

I spy
with my little eye

a pair of
pink socks

Peter Blake, *On the Balcony*

I spy
with my little eye

a black
beetle

Jan van Kessel 1, *Insects*

I spy
with my little eye

a white
moon

René Magritte, *Le Maître d'Ecole*

I spy
with my little eye

a brown
cow

The Nativity from a French Book of Hours

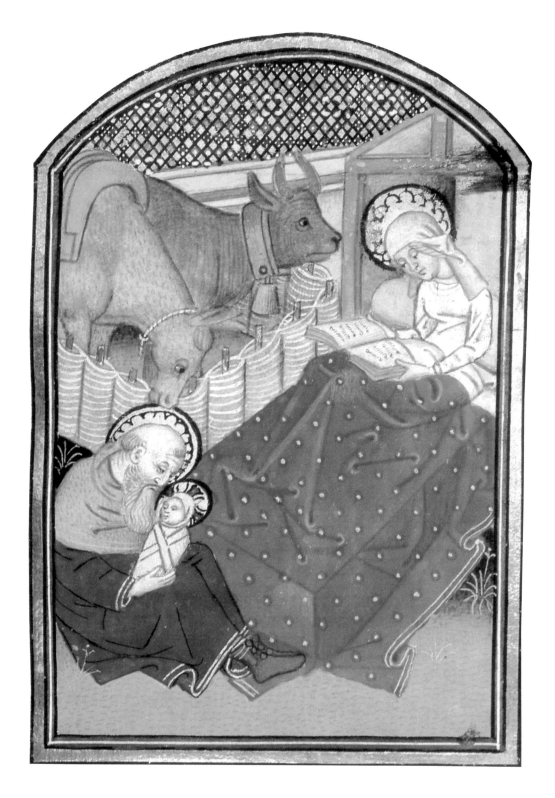

I spy
with my little eye

a silver
spoon

Bernhard Dörries, *Breakfast Still Life*

I spy
with my little eye

a gold bell

Diego Velázquez, *Prince Felipe Próspero*

I spy
with my little eye

lots of
colours

*How many colours
can you spy?*

Michael Craig-Martin, *Eye Test*

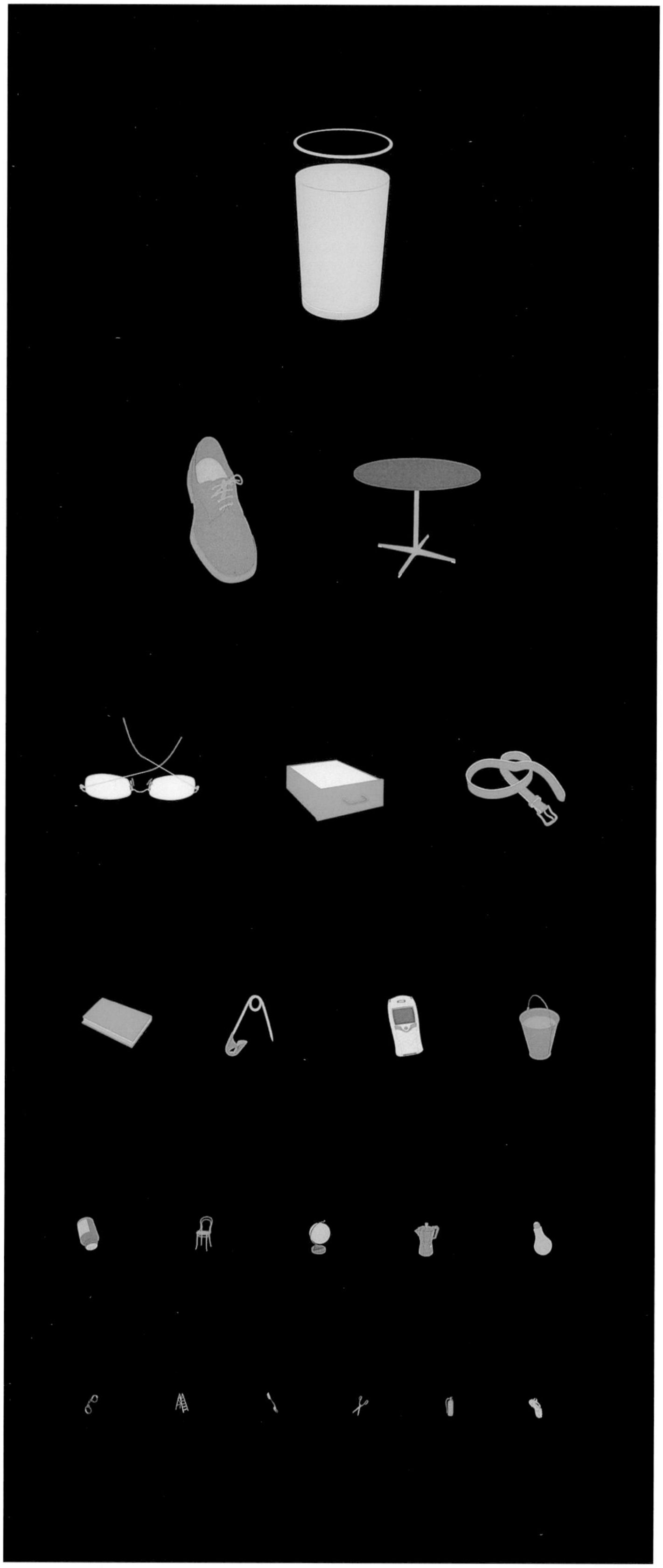

I Spied With My Little Eye

Red

Michael Craig-Martin (born 1941), *Untitled* (1998)

Government Art Collection, London

Yellow

Robert Delaunay (1885-1941), *Rythme No.1* (1938)

Musée Nationale d'Art Moderne, Centre Georges Pompidou, Paris

Blue

Pablo Picasso (1881-1973), *Maya with a Doll* (1938)

Musée Picasso, Paris

Orange

John Frederick Peto (1854-1907), *The Poor Man's Store* (1885)

Museum of Fine Arts, Boston. Gift of Maxim Karolik

Purple

Richard Paul Lohse (1902-1988), *Movement around a Four-squared Centre* (1958-1969)

Kunstmuseum Winterthur, Switzerland

Green

The fabulous region of Himavant from a Burmese manuscript (19th century)

The British Library, London

Grey

Ando Hiroshige (1797-1858), *Fuji from the Sagami River*

The Newark Museum, Newark, New Jersey. John Cotton Dana Collection

Pink

Peter Blake (born 1932), *On the Balcony* (1955-1957)

Tate Gallery, London

Black

Jan van Kessel 1 (1626-1679), *Insects*

The Fitzwilliam Museum, Cambridge

White

René Magritte (1898-1967), *Le Maître d'Ecole* (1955)

Private Collection

Brown

The Nativity from a French Book of Hours (15th century)

The Fitzwilliam Museum, Cambridge

Silver

Bernhard Dörries (1898-1978), *Breakfast Still Life* (1927)

Sprengel Museum, Hanover, Germany

Gold

Diego Velázquez (1599-1660), *Prince Felipe Próspero* (1659)

Kunsthistorisches Museum, Vienna

Many colours

Michael Craig-Martin (born 1941), *Eye Test* (2005)

Private Collection

ACKNOWLEDGEMENTS

The author and publishers would like to thank the galleries, museums, private collectors and copyright holders who have given their permission to reproduce the pictures in this book.

Michael Craig-Martin, *Untitled*: Inv. Nr 17319,
Courtesy of the Government Art Collection (UK) © Michael Craig-Martin and Gagosian Gallery

Robert Delaunay, *Rythme No. 1*: inside and cover, © L&M Services B.V. Amsterdam 20060808

Pablo Picasso, *Maya with a doll*: © Photo RMN/© Jean-Gilles Berizzi. © Succession Picasso/
DACS 2007. HarperCollins has paid DACS' visual creators for the use of their artistic works

John Frederick Peto, *The Poor Man's Store*: Gift of Maxim Karolik for the M. and M. Karolik
Collection of American Paintings, 1815-1865 62.278.
Photograph © 2007 Museum of Fine Arts, Boston

Richard Paul Lohse, *Movement Around a Four-squared Centre*: inside and frontis,
Kunstmuseum Winterthur. Purchase, 1972.
© DACS 2007. HarperCollins has paid DACS' visual creators for the use of their artistic works

The fabulous region of Himavant from a Burmese manuscript: Burmese Buddhist Cosmology/
The British Library, London Or. 14004, f.34 © The British Library, London

Ando Hiroshige, *Fuji from the Sagami River*: Work Collection of The Newark Museum,
John Cotton Dana Collection. Inv: 00.117. Newark, The Newark Museum.
© Photo The Newark Museum/Art Resource/Scala, London

Peter Blake, *On the Balcony*: © TATE, London 2006. © Peter Blake.
Licensed by DACS 2007. HarperCollins has paid DACS'
visual creators for the use of their artistic works

Jan van Kessel 1, *Insects*: Accession Number 309. Reproduction by permission of the Syndics of
The Fitzwilliam Museum, Cambridge

René Magritte, *Le Maître d'Ecole*: © Photothèque R. Magritte - ADAGP, Paris 2006.
© ADAGP, Paris and DACS, London 2007.
HarperCollins has paid DACS' visual creators for the use of their artistic works

The Nativity from a French Book of Hours: MS 69. folio 48 recto.
Reproduction by permission of the Syndics of The Fitzwilliam Museum, Cambridge

First published in Great Britain by HarperCollins Children's Books in 2007

1 3 5 7 9 10 8 6 4 2
ISBN-13: 978-0-00-723400-4   ISBN-10: 0-00-723400-7

Printed and bound in Hong Kong by Printing Express